The Missing Bone

Story by Diana Noonan

Illustrations by Erin Taylor

Contents

Chapter 1

The Big Clear-Out

It was Saturday morning.
Tane and his sister, Kara, were helping Mum and Dad to clear out the old shed in their yard.

That afternoon, a man with a digger was coming to knock down the old shed.
Then there would be room to build a new garage.

Underneath all the junk in the shed,
Tane found an old wooden brush and a pot.

Kara found a pair of glasses and a clock.

"How did these things get in the shed?" Tane asked Mum.

"Long ago," said Mum,
"this shed was your great-grandparents' house."

"The things you found would have belonged to them," said Dad.

“Can we keep them?” asked Kara.

“Yes,” said Dad.

“They’re our family treasures!” said Tane.

Chapter 2

Another Treasure

That afternoon, the family watched while the digger knocked down the shed. Then, a truck came to take away the broken wood.

After that, the digger driver dug up the soil
that was under the shed, and put it in a big pile.
Then he made the ground flat, ready for the new garage.

When the digger had gone,
Tane and Kara had fun
running up and down the pile of soil.

Suddenly, Tane saw something poking out of the pile.
"It looks a bit like a bone," he said. "Let's pull it out."

But it was stuck, deep in the soil.

Kara called Mum and Dad over to help.
Then, everyone pulled together, and out came a gigantic bone.

“Cool!” said Kara.

“It looks like a very old animal bone,” said Mum.

“Now we have another family treasure,” said Tane, smiling.

But Dad shook his head.
“If the bone is very old, it could be important,” he said.
“It might belong in a museum.”

That afternoon, Mum called the museum.

“Someone is coming over on Monday to look at the bone,” she said.

Chapter 3

Straight to the Museum

When Tane and Kara got home from school on Monday, there was a woman in the kitchen with Mum. They were looking at the bone.

"I'm Meera," said the woman, smiling. "I work at the museum. The bone you have found is very special. I would like to take it back to the museum so I can learn more about it."

Tane and Kara felt sad to be losing their treasure.

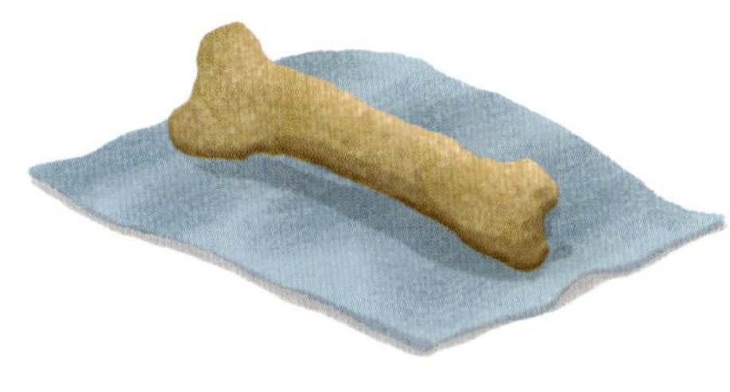

On Friday after school, Mum and Dad had some exciting news.

"We're going straight to the museum," said Mum.
"Meera sent a message to say she has something to show us."

When they arrived at the museum,
Meera was talking to a man with a camera.

"Hello," said Meera, when she saw Tane and Kara.
"This is Daniel from the Palaeontologist* Society.
They have a website all about the bones of animals
that lived thousands of years ago."

*Say: *pay-lee-on-tol-o-jist.*

Meera led the family to a room
full of magnificent animal skeletons.
She stopped beside a very large one.

"This is a moa skeleton," she told Tane and Kara.
"Moa were birds that couldn't fly. Some were huge!
The last moa died more than 500 years ago.
All we have left of them are their bones."

"A piece of that moa skeleton is missing," said Tane, pointing at its leg.

"It's not missing any more!" said Meera, smiling. "Let me explain."

She put on a pair of gloves, then reached into a box and took out a big bone.
"This is the bone that you and Kara found," she said.

"Years ago, all but one piece of this moa skeleton was discovered beside a shallow stream, not far from your house," said Meera.

"The bone you found was probably carried further downstream from that site during a big flood. Over the years, it somehow became buried under soil. Then the shed was built on top of it."

Tane and Kara couldn't stop smiling.

"Would you two like to help me fit the bone into the skeleton?" asked Meera. "Daniel is going to take our photo to put on his group's website."

"Yes, *please*," cried Kara and Tane.

Chapter 4

On the Internet!

After the bone was in place, everybody stood back to admire it.

"The skeleton is perfect, now," said Tane.

"Be sure to look at our website tomorrow," Daniel told Tane and Kara cheerfully. "Your photo will be on it!"

The next day, Tane and Kara looked at the Palaeontologist Society's website. Their photo was there!

"Palaeontologists from all over the world have liked it!" said Tane.
"And some of them want to know more about how we found the bone!"

"I'm glad that the bone is in the museum," said Kara.

"Me, too," said Tane.
"It doesn't belong to our family, after all.
It's a treasure for everyone to share."

"And we can go to see it whenever we want to!"
replied Kara, smiling.